UNCLE VANYA

Scenes from Country Life in Four Acts

by

Anton Chekhov

English Language Version

by

Lynn-Steven Johanson

CAST

ALEXANDRE VLADIMIROVICH SEREBRYAKOV, a retired professor

YELENA ANDREEVNA, his wife, 27

SONYA ALEXANDROVNA, his daughter by his first marriage

MARIA VASILYEVNA, the widowed mother of the Professor's first wife

IVAN PETROVICH VOINITSKY (VANYA), her son

MIKHAIL LVOVICH ASTROV, a doctor

ILYA ILYICH TELEGIN, an impoverished landowner

MARINA, a nurse

WORKMAN

WATCHMAN

The action takes place on Serebryakov's estate.

This version of *Uncle Vanya* was first produced by University Theatre, Western Illinois University, Macomb, Illinois, and opened on October 17, 1990 with the following cast:

SEREBRYAKOV..Sonny Bell
YELENA..Shona Joy
SONYA...Raina Ames
MARIA...Kristin Bohn
VANYA..Mitchell Sparks
ASTROV.. Graham Murphy
TELEGIN..Ted Lynn
MARINA..Danine Schell
WORKMAN...Max Crawford
WATCHMAN..James J. Loula

It was directed by Lynn-Steven Johanson; scenery designed by S. Kent Miller; lighting designed by Brian Quinto; costumes designed by Pamela Crevcoure; and sound designed by Steve Schepker. The stage manager was David A. Ullmann.

ISBN 978-1-300-13573-9

URL: LSJohanson.com
Email: ls-johanson@live.com

for

Sonny Bell

ACT I

SETTING: The garden. Part of the house and the veranda can be seen. Beneath an old poplar tree, a table is set for tea. There are benches and chairs, on one of which lies a guitar. Close to the table there is a swing. It is between two and three o'clock in the afternoon on a cloudy day.

AT RISE: MARINA, a large, slow moving, old woman is sitting near the samovar knitting a stocking. ASTROV paces back and forth near her.

MARINA

(pouring a glass of tea)

Have some tea, my dear.

ASTROV

(reluctantly taking the glass)

I don't really care for any.

MARINA

A little vodka, maybe?

ASTROV

No. I don't drink vodka everyday. Besides, it's too humid.

(pause)

Nanny, how long have we known one another?

MARINA

How long? Oh, Lord, let me see now . . . You first came to this area . . . when was it . . . ? Sonya's mother was still living. You looked in on her for two winters . . . So that makes it eleven years.

(after a moment's pause)

Maybe longer . . .

ASTROV

Have I changed much since then?

MARINA

Quite a bit. You were young and handsome, then. But now you've aged— you're not as good looking as you used to be. And then, you like your vodka, too.

ASTROV

Yes . . . In ten years I've become a different man. Do you know why? I have to work too hard, Nanny. On my feet from morning 'til night, never a moment's rest. And at night I lie under the blankets fearing that I will be hauled out of bed to see another sick person. In all the time we've known one another, I haven't had a single day off. No wonder I've aged. Life is boring, stupid and dirty . . . it drags you down. You're surrounded by the strangest people, all of them just . . . strange. And after you've lived with them for a couple of years, without knowing it, you've become a little strange yourself. It's inevitable.

(twisting his long moustache)

Look how I've grown this huge moustache. How absurd. I've become strange, Nanny. I haven't become stupid yet, thank God. My brain still works, but my feelings have gone numb. I don't want anything, I don't need anything, I don't love anyone except you, Nanny.

(kisses her on the head)

When I was a little boy, I had a nanny just like you.

MARINA

Would you like something to eat?

ASTROV

No. During the third week of Lent I went over to Malitzkoye. There was an epidemic . . . typhus . . . The huts were crowded with sick people. Dirt and smoke everywhere. And the stench calves lying on the floor with the sick, little pigs running about. I worked all day long without so much as a bite to eat. And when I got home, they still wouldn't let me rest. They carried in a switchman from the railroad. I put him on the table to operate, and he dies on me under the chloroform. And just when I least wanted it, my feelings chose to wake up, and my conscience began to haunt me as if I had killed him deliberately. I sat down, closed my eyes like this, and I thought: those people who will be living one or two hundred years from now, will they have a good word for us? I doubt if they will, Nanny. We'll be forgotten.

MARINA

People may forget but God never will.

ASTROV

Thank you. That was well said.

(VOINITSKY comes out of the house. He has had a nap after lunch and looks rumpled. He sits down on the bench and adjusts his stylish necktie.)

VOINITSKY

Yes . . .

(pause)

Yes . . .

ASTROV

Have a good sleep?

VOINITSKY

Yes . . . very good.

(yawns)

Since the professor and his wife came to live here, there's been utter chaos. I sleep at odd hours, eat fancy lunches and fancy dinners, drink wine—it's not healthy. Before they came, I never had any time to myself. Sonya and I worked hard all day . . . But now only Sonya works while I sleep, eat and drink . . . it's not good.

MARINA

It's shameful. The professor doesn't wake up till noon but the samovar has been boiling all morning waiting for him. Before they came, we always had dinner shortly after noon like everyone else. Now it's nearly seven. At night the professor sits up reading and writing. Then, suddenly, at two o'clock in the morning, he rings. Good heavens, what is it? He wants tea! So you have to wake the servants, heat the samovar . . . it's shameful!

ASTROV

Are they going to stay much longer?

VOINITSKY

(whistling)

A hundred years. The professor has decided to settle here.

MARINA

It goes on and on look here. The samovar's been on the table two hours, and they've gone for a walk.

VOINITSKY

They're coming. They're coming. Now don't get upset.

(Voices are heard. SEREBRYAKOV, YELENA, SONYA and TELEGIN enter from the far end of the garden as they return from their walk.)

SEREBRYAKOV

Beautiful, just beautiful . . . what scenery.

TELEGIN

Yes, sir. The view is remarkable.

SONYA

Tomorrow we'll go to the forest reserve. Would you like that, Papa?

VOINITSKY

Let's have some tea.

SEREBRYAKOV

My friends, please have my tea brought to the study. I have some more work to do today.

SONYA

I'm sure you'll like it at the reserve.

(YELENA, SEREBRYAKOV and SONYA into the house. TELEGIN goes to the table and sits down by MARINA.)

VOINITSKY

It's hot and humid, yet our great scholar goes for a walk in an overcoat, galoshes, gloves and umbrella.

ASTROV

Obviously he takes good care of himself.

VOINITSKY

Isn't she lovely? Absolutely lovely. I've never seen a more beautiful woman in all my life.

TELEGIN

Marina Timofeyevna, whether I ride through the open fields, take a walk through the shady garden or simply look at this table, I feel so very happy. The weather is delightful, the birds are singing, and we are living in peace and harmony. What more do we need?

(taking a glass of tea)

Thank you. You're most kind.

VOINITSKY

(dreamily)

Her eyes . . . what a marvelous woman!

ASTROV

Tell us something, Ivan Petrovich.

VOINITSKY

(listlessly)

Tell you what?

ASTROV

Isn't there anything new?

VOINITSKY

Nothing. It's the same old story. If anything I'm worse since I've grown lazy and do nothing but grumble like an old grouch. Mama jabbers like a magpie about the emancipation of women. She has one eye on the grave and studies her books with the other, searching for the dawn of a new life.

ASTROV

And the professor?

VOINITSKY

The professor continues to sit in his study, writing from morning until late into the night. I feel sorry for the paper he writes on! He'd do better to write his autobiography. What a magnificent subject! A retired professor, a dried fish with a doctorate . . . Suffering from gout, rheumatism, migraine and a liver swollen with jealousy and envy . . . This old codfish lives on his first wife's estate. He doesn't want to, of course, but he can't afford to live in town. He complains constantly about his misfortunes, when in reality, he has been most fortunate.

(nervously)

Think how lucky he's been. The son of a common sexton, he studied theology and managed to obtain various degrees and a professorship. Then he became one of the "elite", the son-in-law of a Senator and so on and so forth. But that's not important. My point is this. For twenty-five years the man has been reading and writing about art and he understands nothing whatsoever about it. For twenty-five years he has been chewing over other people's ideas about realism, naturalism and other nonsense; twenty-five years he's been lecturing and writing about things intelligent people already know and stupid people aren't interested in. All this means is that for twenty-five years he has been pouring from an empty pot! But, oh what an opinion he has of himself! What pretensions. Now he's retired and not a soul has ever heard of him. He's a complete unknown. So, for twenty-five years he's held a position which rightfully belonged to someone else. But yet, he struts about like a god.

ASTROV

Well, I think you're jealous.

VOINITSKY

Yes, I am jealous. And his success with women! Don Juan pales by comparison. My sister, his first wife, a beautiful, gentle creature, as pure as the sky is blue, noble, generous, and with more admirers than he had students. She loved him as only angels can love beings as pure as themselves. Our mother worships the ground he walks on. His second wife, a beautiful, intelligent woman—you've just seen her—married him when he was already an old man. She gave him her youth and beauty, her freedom, radiance. Why? For what?

ASTROV

Is she faithful to the professor?

VOINITSKY

Yes, unfortunately.

ASTROV

What do you mean, "unfortunately".

VOINITSKY

Her fidelity is false from beginning to end. It's full of rhetoric but it makes no sense. Deceiving an old husband you can't stand, that's immoral; but stifling your very youth, your feelings and vitality, that's not immoral at all.

TELEGIN

(in a tearful voice)

I don't like it when you talk this way. Well . . . Anyone who would deceive a wife or husband is someone who cannot be trusted, someone who could very well betray his own country.

VOINITSKY

(annoyed)

Oh, turn off the spigot, Waffles!

TELEGIN

Please, Vanya. Let me speak. My wife ran away with a man she loved the day after we were married because of my unattractive appearance. But I have never failed in my duty. I still love her, I'm still faithful to her, I help her however I can. I've given up everything I own to educate the children she had by this man. I've lost my happiness, but I still have my pride. And what about her? Her youth is gone, her beauty has faded with time, the man she loved is dead. What does she have left?

(SONYA and YELENA enter. A little later, MARIA VASILYEVNA enters carrying a book. She sits down and reads. She is served tea and drinks it without looking up.)

SONYA

(to MARINA, hurriedly)

Nanny, some peasants from the village have come. Go see what they want. I'll take care of the tea.

(SONYA pours the tea. MARINA leaves. YELENA takes a glass of tea and drinks it sitting on the swing.)

ASTROV

I came here to see your husband, you know. You wrote saying he was quite ill—rheumatism and something else—but he appears to be perfectly well.

YELENA

Last evening he was depressed and complained about pains in his legs. But today he seems better . . .

ASTROV

And I galloped twenty miles at breakneck speed to get here. Well, never mind, it's not the first time. I'll just stay the night, now that I'm here. At least I'll get some sleep.

SONYA

That's wonderful. It's so seldom you stay with us. I don't suppose you've had anything to eat?

ASTROV

No, I haven't.

SONYA

Then you'll have to join us for dinner, too. We never dine much before seven these days.

(drinks her tea)

The tea is cold!

TELEGIN

The temperature of the samovar has dropped quite a bit.

YELENA

It's all right, Ivan Ivanovich. We'll just drink it cold.

TELEGIN

Excuse me . . . my name is Ilya Ilyich not Ivan Ivanovich. Sorry. Ilya Ilyich Telegin, or "Waffles", as some people call me because of my pock- marked face. I am Sonya's godfather, you see, and the professor, your husband, knows me well. I live here on the estate . . . You may have noticed me. I have dinner with you everyday.

SONYA

Ilya Ilyich is our helper, our right hand.

(tenderly)

Here, let me pour you some more tea, Godfather.

MARIA

Oh!

SONYA

What's the matter, mother?

MARIA VASILYEVNA

I forgot to tell Alexandre . . . I'm losing my memory . . . I received a letter today from Pavel Alekseyevich in Kharkov. He sent his new pamphlet.

ASTROV

Is it interesting?

MARIA VASILYEVNA

Yes . . . it's interesting . . . but rather odd. He's attacking the very thing he himself was defending seven years ago. It's terrible.

VOINITSKY

There's nothing terrible about that. Drink your tea, Maman.

MARIA VASILYEVNA

But I want to talk.

VOINITSKY

We've been talking and talking and reading pamphlets for fifty years. It's time we stop.

MARIA VASILYEVNA

For some reason, you don't care for the sound of my voice. I'll tell you something, Jean. In the last year, you've changed so much I hardly recognize you anymore. You used to be a man with strong convictions, an inspiring example . . .

VOINITSKY

Oh, yes. An inspiring example who inspired no one.

(pause)

An inspiring example. What a vicious joke. I am forty-seven years old. Up until last year I deliberately tried to blind myself just like you blind yourself with all your academic theories in order to avoid seeing life as it is, and I thought I was doing the right thing. But now, if you only knew! I don't sleep at night because I'm so angry and frustrated over wasting my life. I could have had everything. Now I'm too old.

SONYA

Uncle Vanya, this is boring.

MARIA VASILYEVNA

(to her son)

You seem to be blaming your former convictions for something or other . . . They're not to blame, you are. Convictions in and of themselves mean nothing. You should have done something.

VOINITSKY

Done something? Not everyone can be a perpetual writing machine like your Herr Professor!

MARIA VASILYEVNA

What do you mean by that?

SONYA

(pleading)

Grandmother! Uncle Vanya! Please!

VOINITSKY

I'll be quiet. I'll be quiet . . . and I apologize.

(pause)

YELENA

Lovely day today . . . not too hot.

(pause)

VOINITSKY

A lovely day to hang one's self.

(TELEGIN tunes the guitar. MARINA walks near the house calling the chickens.)

MARINA

Chick, chick, chick.

SONYA

Nanny, what did those peasants want?

MARINA

Oh, the same old thing, that small plot of waste ground. Here chick, chick, chick.

SONYA

Which one are you looking for?

MARINA

The speckled hen. She's gone off somewhere with her chicks. I don't want the crows to get them.

(MARINA goes out. TELEGIN begins playing a polka. They all listen in silence. A WORKMAN enters.)

WORKMAN

Is the doctor here?

(to ASTROV)

Excuse me, sir, but they've come for you.

ASTROV

Where from?

WORKMAN

The factory.

ASTROV

(annoyed)

Thank you. Well . . . I'll have to go.

(looks around for his cap)

Damn it. What a nuisance.

SONYA

It's aggravating, I know. But come back for dinner when you've finished.

ASTROV

No, it will be too late.

(to the WORKMAN)

Do me a favor, would you? Get me a glass of vodka.

(WORKMAN leaves; ASTROV finds his cap.)

In one of Ostrovsky's plays, there is a man with a large moustache and small abilities. That's me. Well, goodbye everyone. If you would care to look in on me some time—you could accompany Sonya there. It would give me real pleasure. I have a small estate, eighty acres or so, but if you're interested, there's a model garden and nursery. You won't find another like it for hundreds of miles around. Next to me is the state forest reserve. The forester is old and in bad health, so I've been running things.

YELENA

Yes, I've been told you have a great love for the forests. That's a valuable service, of course, but doesn't it interfere with your real work. After all, you are a doctor.

ASTROV

Only God knows what our real life's work is.

YELENA

And is it interesting?

ASTROV

Oh, yes. The work is interesting.

VOINITSKY

(ironically)

Very.

YELENA

(to ASTROV)

You're still a young man. You look what . . . thirty-six, thirty-seven . . . it can't be all that interesting. Just trees, trees and more trees. Surely that gets monotonous.

SONYA

No, it's fascinating. The doctor plants new forests every year. He's been given a bronze medal and a citation for his work. He's been doing all he can to save the remaining forests. If you'd listen to what he says, you'd understand. He says the forests beautify the earth, they teach man to appreciate beauty and be aware of its overall majesty. Forests soften the harshness of the climate. And in countries with milder climates, people spend less time struggling against nature; they become softer and more gentle. People in those places are beautiful and exciting, sensitive and passionate, their speech is elegant and their movements are graceful. The arts and sciences flourish among them, their attitude is never somber and they treat women with courtesy and respect.

VOINITSKY

(laughing)

Bravo! Bravo! . . This is all very nice but not very convincing.

(to ASTROV)

I hope you will allow me, my friend, to continue burning logs in my stoves and building barns out of wood.

ASTROV

You can burn peat in you stoves and build your barns out of stone. Look, I admit that it's necessary to cut trees to meet our needs, but do we have to destroy entire forests? The Russian forests are practically groaning under the axe; millions of trees are lost; the homes for countless animals and birds have disappeared; rivers are drying up; wonderful landscapes have vanished forever. And its all because man is too lazy and stupid to bend down and pick up his fuel from the earth.

(to YELENA)

Isn't that true? Only an utter barbarian could burn beauty like that in a stove and destroy what can never be replaced. Man is endowed with reason and creative power to increase what is given to him, but up until now he has done nothing to create but everything to destroy. The forests are getting fewer and fewer, the rivers only trickle with water, wildlife is becoming extinct, the climate is ruined and the earth becomes uglier and poorer every day.

(to VOINITSKY)

You sit there with an ironic look on your face. You don't take me seriously, and . . . and maybe its just another one of my eccentric ideas, but when I pass by the forest of a peasant, the forest I saved from the axe, or when I hear the rustling of the trees I planted with my own hands, then I know that I am making a slight contribution toward controlling the climate and if, in a thousand years, man is happier, in some minute way I will have been responsible. When I plant a birch tree and later see its branches filled with leaves and swaying in the wind, my heart fills with pride and I . . .

(seeing the WORKMAN enter with a glass of vodka on a tray)

However . . .

(drinks)

I must go. This is all probably some crazy idea, anyway. Goodbye!

(ASTROV goes toward the house.)

SONYA

(takes his arm and goes with him)

When will you come see us again?

ASTROV

I don't know.

SONYA

Not for another month?

(WORKMAN exits. ASTROV and SONYA go into the house.)
(MARIA VASILYEVNA and TELEGIN remain at the table. YELENA and VOINITSKY walk toward the porch.)

YELENA

Ivan Petrovich, you have been impossible again. Did you have to irritate your mother with talk about "perpetual writing machines?" And today at lunch, you had another argument with Alexandre. This is all so petty.

VOINITSKY

But what if I hate him?

YELENA

You have no reason to hate him. He's the same as everyone else. No worse than you.

VOINITSKY

If you could only see your face, the way you move. Life seems like such an effort for you . . . just so much to bear.

YELENA

Yes, so much to bear and so boring. Everyone criticizes my husband, everyone looks at me with pity. Oh, the poor thing, her husband is such an old man! This concern for me I understand it all too well. It's the same as what Astrov said a moment ago: you wantonly destroy the forests, all of you, and soon there will be nothing left on this earth. You do the same thing with people, wantonly destroy them, and soon, thanks to you, there will be no loyalty, purity or capacity for self-sacrifice left either. Why is it you're unable to show indifference toward women who don't belong to you? I'll tell you, the doctor was right. There's a demon of destruction deep inside all of you. You have no pity whatever for forests, birds, women or even each other.

VOINITSKY

I don't like this sort of philosophy.

YELENA

The doctor, he has an interesting face weary . . . and tense. I think Sonya finds him attractive. She's in love with him, and I can see why. He's come to the house three times since I arrived, but I'm rather shy and haven't taken the opportunity to talk with him or be friendly to him. He probably thinks I'm conceited. It's entirely possible, Ivan Petrovich, that the reason you and I are friends is because we are such frightfully boring people. Don't look at me like that. I don't like it.

VOINITSKY

How else can I look at you? I love you. You're my happiness, my life, my youth. I know there is little or no chance of your returning my feelings. But I don't want anything. Just let me look at you and listen to your voice . . .

YELENA

Shush! Someone might hear you!

(They walk toward the house.)

VOINITSKY

(following her)

Let me talk about my love, don't drive me away . . . that will be the ultimate happiness for me . . .

YELENA

This is torture . . .

(They both go into the house. TELEGIN plucks the guitar and plays a polka. MARIA VASILYEVNA makes notes in the margin of her pamphlet.)

CURTAIN

ACT II

SCENE: The dining room of Serebryakov's house. It is night.

AT RISE: The WATCHMAN can be heard tapping in the garden. SEREBRYAKOV is sitting in an armchair in front of an open window dozing. YELENA sits beside him, also dozing.

SEREBRYAKOV

(awakening)

Who's there? Sonya, is it you?

YELENA

It's me.

SEREBRYAKOV

Oh, Yelena. . . these pains are unbearable.

YELENA

Your blanket has fallen on the floor.

(wraps it around his legs)

I'll shut the window Alexandre.

SEREBRYAKOV

No, please. I'm suffocating. I dozed off and dreamed that my left leg belonged to someone else. Then these terrible pains woke me up. It's not like gout, it must be rheumatism. What time is it?

YELENA

Half past twelve.

(pause)

SEREBRYAKOV

Tomorrow morning, go to the library and try to find a Batyushkov. I think we have one.

YELENA

Here?

SEREBRYAKOV

The Batyushkov . . . the volume of works by Batyushkov I remember we had it once. Why am I having so much trouble breathing?

YELENA

You're tired. You haven't slept for two nights, now.

SEREBRYAKOV

They say Turgenev had gout and it turned into angina. I'm afraid the same thing will happen to me. Damn old age, to hell with it. I hate it. Since I've grown old, I find myself repulsive. I'm sure all of you must find me disgusting.

YELENA

You talk about your old age as if it was all our fault.

SEREBYRAKOV

You find me the most disgusting of all, don't you.

(YELENA gets up and sits farther away from him.)

SEREBRYAKOV

You're right, of course. I'm no fool, I understand. You're young, healthy, beautiful. You want to live. I'm an old man, practically a corpse. I understand. I do. It's absurd that I'm still alive really. But just wait a while. Soon I'll set all of you free. I won't drag it out much longer.

YELENA

I'm very tired. For God's sake, be quiet.

SEREBRYAKOV

It seems everyone is tired . . . tired, bored, wasting their youth on my account while I am the only one who's enjoying himself. Yes, of course!

YELENA

Stop it. You've worn me out.

SEREBRYAKOV

I've worn everyone out. Of course.

YELENA

(through tears)

I can't take this any longer! Just . . . what is it you want?

SEREBRYAKOV

Nothing.

YELENA

Then I beg you, please be quiet.

SEREBRYAKOV

It's a strange thing. Ivan Petrovich opens his mouth or that brainless mother of his begins babbling away, it's all right, everyone listens. But if I say so much as a word, everyone begins to feel miserable. Even the sound of my voice offends them. Well, maybe I am offensive. I'm egotistical, a tyrant. So what? Haven't I the right to a little conceit in my old age? Haven't I earned it? Now I ask you, haven't I a right to some peace and quiet, to some attention from people?

YELENA

No one is disputing your rights.

(window bangs in the wind)

The wind has come up, I'd better shut the window.

(shutting the window)

It's going to rain. No one is disputing your rights.

(Pause. The WATCHMAN in the garden is heard tapping his stick and singing a song.)

SEREBRYAKOV

You devote your life to learning, you grow accustomed to your study, to the lecture halls, to your distinguished colleagues. Then suddenly, for seemingly no reason, you find yourself in this tomb, watching stupid people everyday, listening to their trivial chatter! . . . I want to live, I love success, I like being well-known and making a stir. But here, I might as well be in exile in Siberia. To spend all your time yearning for the past, watching others succeed, constantly in fear of dying . . . I just can't do it. I don't have the strength. And to make matters worse, people won't even forgive me for growing old.

YELENA

Be patient. In five or six years I'll be old too.

(SONYA enters)

SONYA

Papa, you were the one who made us send for Doctor Astrov. But now that he's here, you won't let him see you. That's very inconsiderate. We've bothered him for nothing.

SEREBRYAKOV

What can your Astrov do for me? He knows as much about medicine as I do about astronomy.

SONYA

We can't send for an entire medical faculty just to treat your gout.

SEREBRYAKOV

Well, I'm not going to talk to that damned fool.

SONYA

Suit yourself.

(She sits)

It makes no difference to me.

SEREBRYAKOV

What time is it now?

YELENA

It's going on one.

SEREBRYAKOV

I'm suffocating Sonya, give me the drops on the table.

SONYA

Here.

(handing him the drops)

SEREBRYAKOV

(irritable)

No-no. Not those! It's no use asking for anything.

SONYA

Don't be so temperamental. Some people may be amused by it but I'm not, so behave yourself. I don't have time for this. I have to get up early and see to the hay mowing.

(VOINITSKY enters wearing a robe and carrying a candle.)

VOINITSKY

We're going to get a storm.

(lightning flashes)

You see? Yelena, Sonya go to bed. I'll take over for you.

SEREBRYAKOV

(alarmed)

No, no. Don't leave me alone with him. He'll talk me to death!

VOINITSKY

You have to let them rest. They've gone two nights now with no sleep.

SEREBRYAKOV

Let them go to bed, but you go away too. I thank you, but please. For the sake of our past friendship, don't argue. We'll talk some other time.

VOINITSKY

(smiling ironically)

Our past friendship. . . Past. . .

SONYA

Be quiet Uncle Vanya.

SEREBRYAKOV

(to his wife)

My dear, don't leave me with him. It's windy enough outside.

VOINITSKY

This is getting ridiculous.

(MARINA enters carrying a candle.)

SONYA

Nanny, you ought to be in bed. It's late.

MARINA

The samovar's still on the table. I can't very well go to bed.

SEREBRYAKOV

Everyone is awake, everyone is worn to a frazzle. Except for me, of course. I'm in a state of bliss!

MARINA

(going up to SEREBRYAKOV, gently)

What's the matter, my dear? Does it hurt? I have pains in my legs, too. Throbbing pains.

(straightening his blanket)

You've had this problem for a long time. Sonya's mother, God rest her soul, used to stay up night after night worrying about it . . . She just thought the world of you . . .

(pause)

Old people are just like children. All they want is a little attention. But nobody cares about old people.

(She kisses SEREBRYAKOV on the shoulder.)

Come to bed now, my dear . . . Come along now . . . I'll give you some lime flower tea and warm your feet . . . I'll say a prayer for you.

SEREBRYAKOV

(moved)

Let's go then, Marina.

MARINA

My legs hurt too. They just throb, it's terrible.

(MARINA leads SEREBRYAKOV with SONYA's help.)

Sonya's mother used to get so upset, worried herself sick . . . crying all the time. You were just a little girl then, Sonya. You didn't understand . . . That's it, come along now.

(SEREBRYAKOV, SONYA and MARINA exit.)

YELENA

He's worn me out. I can hardly stand up.

VOINITSKY

He's worn you out. I've worn myself out. This is the third night I've gone without sleep.

YELENA

Things have gotten so out of hand in this house. Your mother hates everything except her pamphlets and the professor; the professor is so irritable he doesn't trust me, and he's afraid of you; Sonya's angry with her father as well as with me. She hasn't spoken to me in two weeks; you hate my husband and openly despise your own mother; I'm so on edge, I must have been on the verge of tears twenty times today . . . A fine state of affairs.

VOINITSKY

Let's leave the philosophizing out of it.

YELENA

Ivan Petrovich, you are an educated, intelligent man. Surely you must realize that the world is being destroyed, not by fire and war, but by malice and hatred in all this petty quarreling. You should stop grumbling and work out some sort of reconciliation.

VOINITSKY

First of all, reconcile me to myself. My love . . .

(He presses her hand to his lips.)

YELENA

Stop it!

(pulls her hand away)

Go away!

VOINITSKY

The rain will soon be over and everything in nature will revive and breathe freely again. Everything except me. Day and night the same thought haunts me like some evil spirit, the thought that my life has been hopelessly wasted. I have no past. It was thrown away on things of no importance. The present is so unbearable that it borders on the absurd. There you are: my life and my love. Where do they belong? What should I do with them? My feelings are being wasted like a ray of sunlight falling on a bottomless pit. I'm simply wasting away.

YELENA

When you talk to me of your love . . . I feel nothing I'm numb and words fail me. I'm sorry, there's nothing I can say to you.

(starting to go)

Good night.

VOINITSKY

(blocking her way)

If you only knew how much it hurts me to know that in this house another life is being wasted. It's yours! What are you waiting for? What foolish idea is holding you back? You have to understand that it's—

YELENA

(staring at him)

Ivan Petrovich, you're drunk!

VOINITSKY

Possibly. Possibly.

YELENA

Where's the doctor?

VOINITSKY

In there . . . He's spending the night in my room. Possibly, possibly . . . Anything is possible!

YELENA

Drinking again today! Why do you do it?

VOINITSKY

To give me the illusion of being alive. Don't try to stop me, Yelena!

YELENA

You never used to drink, and you never used to talk so much . . . Go to bed! You bore me.

VOINITSKY

(kisses her hand)

My dear . . . What a wonderful woman.

YELENA

(annoyed)

Leave me alone! This is disgusting.

(YELENA exits.)

VOINITSKY

(alone)

She's gone . . .

(pause)

Ten years ago I used to meet her at my sister's house. She was seventeen and I was thirty-seven. Why didn't I fall in love with her then and ask her to marry me? It would have been so easy. She'd be my wife now . . . Yes . . . And tonight the storm would have awakened us. She would have been frightened of the thunder, and I would have held her in my arms and whispered, "Don't be afraid, I'm here." Oh, what a wonderful thought. So delightful I can hardly keep from laughing . . . Oh, God, my thoughts are spinning . . . Why am I so old? Why doesn't she understand me? All that rhetoric and idle moralizing, those silly ideas about the world being destroy- ed. I find it all so utterly detestable.

(pause)

How could I have been such a fool, a dupe! I used to worship the professor, that pathetic, gout-riddled old man . . . and I worked like an ox for him. Sonya and I have squeezed every possible drop from this estate. We haggled like a couple of peasants over the prices for our peas, vegetable oil and cheese curd. We did without just so we could save enough kopecks to make a ruble. And we sent him rubles by the thousand. I was proud of him and his great learning. I lived and breathed that man. Everything he wrote, every phrase he spoke seemed to be touched by genius . . . But now, dear God . . . he retires and the sum total of his life comes to light. Not a single page of his work will remain when he's gone. He's absolutely unknown, he's nothing! And I've been cheated. I can see it so clearly . . . duped . . . like a fool.

(ASTROV enters wearing a frock coat but without a waistcoat or tie. He is slightly drunk. He is followed by TELEGIN who carries a guitar.)

ASTROV

Play!

TELEGIN

Everyone's asleep.

ASTROV

Play!

(TELEGIN strums softly to VOINITSKY.)

Are you alone? No ladies?

(Puts hands on his hips and sings softly.)

"Dance my house and dance my bed,
There's no place for the master to lay his head."
The storm woke me up. Nice rain. What time is it?

VOINITSKY

Damned if I know.

ASTROV

I thought I heard Yelena Andreevna's voice.

VOINITSKY

She was here a moment ago.

ASTROV

A very attractive woman.

(examines medicine bottles on the table.)

Medicines. Quite a variety labels . . . from Kharkov, Moscow, Tula. Every city in Russia must have intimate knowledge of this man's gout. Is he ill or just pretending?

VOINITSKY

He's ill.

(pause)

ASTROV

Why are you so moody? Feeling sorry for the professor, maybe?

VOINITSKY

Leave me alone.

ASTROV

Or are you in love with the professor's wife?

VOINITSKY

She's my friend.

ASTROV

Already?

VOINITSKY

What do you mean, "already"?

ASTROV

A woman can become a man's friend only in the following stages: first, an acquaintance; next, a mistress; and finally, a friend.

VOINITSKY

That's a vulgar philosophy.

ASTROV

Well . . . yes. I suppose it is. I must confess that I'm gradually becoming a vulgarian at heart. You see, I'm even drunk. I make it a point to get drunk like this once a month. It makes me arrogant, brash and . . . well, there's nothing I can't do. I undertake the most difficult operations and execute them with the greatest finesse; I draw up the most far-reaching plans for the future; at times like this I no longer think of myself as eccentric. I believe I'm rendering a tremendous service for mankind. Tremendous! At times like this, I have my own systematic philosophy, and all of you, my friends, appear to me like tiny insects . . . or microbes.

(to TELEGIN)

Play, Waffles.

TELEGIN

I'd be happy to, my old friend, with all my heart, but everyone in the house is asleep.

ASTROV

Play!

(TELEGIN strums softly)

Let's have a drink. Come on, I think there's some cognac left. As soon as it's daylight, we'll go to my place. "Zadda right?" I have an assistant who can't seem to say, "Is that all right?" Instead it's always "Zadda right?". . . God he's obnoxious. Well, "Zadda right?"

(sees SONYA entering)

Excuse me, I'm not wearing my tie.

(ASTROV leaves quickly, followed by TELEGIN.)

SONYA

Uncle Vanya, you've been drinking with the doctor again. You make a fine pair. He's always ready for a binge. But it's so unlike you. Why do you do it? It's not very becoming at your age.

VOINITSKY

Age has nothing to do with it. When a person has no life, he must live with illusions. It's better than nothing.

SONYA

All the hay has been mowed, and with the rain every day, it's lying there rotting. And you are living with illusions. You've completely abandoned this estate. I'm doing everything myself and I'm nearly worn out . . .

(alarmed)

Uncle, you have tears in your eyes!

VOINITSKY

Tears? Not at all, that's nonsense . . . The way you looked at me just now reminded me so much of your dear mother. My dear.

(eagerly kisses her hands and face)

My sister . . . my dear sister . . . Where is she now? If she only knew. Oh, if she only knew!

SONYA

What, Uncle? Knew what?

VOINITSKY

It's painful . . . it's not right . . . Never mind . . . Later . . . it's nothing . . . I'm going now.

(He exits.)

SONYA

(knocking at the door)

Mikhail Lvovich! You're not sleeping are you? Could you come in here a moment?

ASTROV

(through the door)

Coming.

(A moment later he enters wearing a waistcoat and tie.)

What can I do for you?

SONYA

You're free to drink if you don't find it disgusting. But don't encourage my uncle, please. It's bad for him.

ASTROV

All right. We won't drink anymore.

(pause)

I'm leaving now. Everything is settled. By the time they finish hitching up the horses, it will be light.

SONYA

It's still raining. Wait until morning.

ASTROV

The storm's almost past. I'll only catch the edge of it. I'm going. And please don't call me again to treat your father. I tell him it's gout, and he tells me it's rheumatism; I tell him to lie down, and he sits up. Today, he refused to even speak to me.

SONYA

He's spoiled.

(looks in the sideboard.)

Would you like something to eat?

ASTROV

Yes. Thank you.

SONYA

I love little late night snacks. I think there's some food in the sideboard. People have remarked that Father had great success with women in his day. Women just spoiled him. Here, have some cheese.

(Both stand at the sideboard and eat.)

ASTROV

I didn't eat anything today just drank. Your father is a difficult man.

(getting a bottle out of the sideboard)

May I?

(pours a glass)

There's no one here, so I can be honest with you. I don't think I could survive a month in your house. I'd suffocate in this atmosphere . . . Your father's preoccupied with his gout and his books; Uncle Vanya with his depression; your grandmother, and then of course, your stepmother.

SONYA

What about my stepmother?

ASTROV

Everything about a human being should be beautiful: face, clothing, mind and soul. She's beautiful, no doubt about that, but . . . all she ever does is eat, sleep, go for walks, and charm us with her beauty. She has no responsibilities, other people work for her . . . Isn't that so? There's no virtue in an idle life.

(pause)

Well, maybe I'm being too severe. I'm dissatisfied with life, like your Uncle Vanya, and we're both becoming a couple of grumblers.

SONYA

Are you really that dissatisfied with life?

ASTROV

I love life in general, but our narrow, provincial Russian life—I can't bear it. I despise it from the depths of my soul. As for my personal life, God knows there's nothing good about that. You know what it's like when you're walking through a forest on a dark night and you see a glimmer of light off in the distance? You don't notice how tired you are or how unsettling the darkness is, not even the thorny branches lashing your face . . . I work harder than anyone in the district, you know that, and it's not easy. Life is insufferable sometimes . . . But the sad thing is . . . I have no glimmer of light in the distance. I have no hopes for myself, no real feelings for other people . . . I haven't really loved anyone in a long, long time.

SONYA

No one at all?

ASTROV

No one. I do happen to be fond of your nanny, but that's for old time's sake. The peasants are all the same—backward, living in the most squalid conditions; it's difficult to get along with the intelligentsia. They tire you out. All of them, all of our good friends are so shallow and petty that they are incapable of seeing past their own noses. The fact is, they're just plain stupid. And the ones who are more intelligent and vigorous indulge themselves with self-analysis and introspection. They whine, hate and slander one another. They'll sneak around, look at a man out of the corner of their eyes and conclude: "Oh, he's a psychopath!" or "He's a windbag." And when they can't think of a label to stick on me they say, "He's a strange one, isn't he? Very strange!" I love the forests, that's strange. I don't eat meat, that's strange, too. They are totally incapable of relating to nature or to people in a direct, honest, open manner. That's all a thing of the past.

(about to have a drink)

SONYA

(stopping him)

No, I beg you, don't drink anymore.

ASTROV

Why not?

SONYA

It's not like you. You're so refined, your voice is soft and gentle . . . And more than that, you're not like all the other people I know. You're special. Why do you want to act like ordinary people who drink and play cards? Don't be like them, I beg you! You always say that people never create; they just destroy what God has given them. So, why on earth are you destroying yourself? Why? You mustn't. You mustn't, I'm begging you, please.

ASTROV

(holds out his hand to her)

I won't drink anymore.

SONYA

Give me your word.

ASTROV

My word of honor.

SONYA

(presses his hand warmly)

Thank you.

ASTROV

Enough! I'm no longer drunk. You see, I'm stone cold sober, and I'll stay that way till the end of my days.

(looks at his watch)

So . . . Let's continue our conversation, shall we? As I was saying, my time is past, it's too late for me, now . . . I'm getting old, I've worked myself too hard, and unfortunately, I've become vulgar, calloused and unable to establish close ties with another person. I don't love anyone . . . and I probably never will. But the one thing that still intrigues me is beauty. I'm not indifferent to that. I think that if she wanted to, Yelena Andreevna could turn my head in a day . . . but that isn't love of course, or affection . . .

(ASTROV covers his eyes with his hands and shudders.)

SONYA

What's the matter?

ASTROV

Nothing . . . During Lent one of my patients died under chloroform.

SONYA

It's time you forgot about that.

(pause)

Tell me, Mikhail Lvovich . . . If I had a friend or a younger sister, and you found out that she . . . well, that she was in love with you. What would you do?

ASTROV

(shrugging his shoulders)

I don't know. I probably wouldn't do anything. I would certainly make it clear that I could never love her . . . and that I have other things weighing on my mind. Well, if I'm going to get home, I'd better leave. I'll say goodbye now, my dear. If we keep talking, I could be here till noon.

(holding her hand)

I'll go out through the drawing room, if I may. I'm afraid your uncle may be further cause for delay.

(ASTROV exits.)

SONYA

He didn't say anything to me . . . His heart and mind are still hidden from me . . . So why do I feel so happy?

(laughs with happiness)

I said, "You're so refined, your voice is soft and gentle . . . " Was it wrong to say such things? His voice vibrates and caresses . . . I can still feel it in the air. But when I told him about a younger sister's feelings, he didn't understand . . .

(wringing her hands)

It's horrible not to be beautiful. Just horrible. And I know I'll never be anything but plain. I know it, I know it . . . Last Sunday as I was walking out of church, I overheard some women talking about me. One of them said, "She's such a kind and generous girl. It's a pity she's so plain." So plain . . .

(YELENA enters.)

YELENA

(opening the window)

The storm is over. The air is so fresh.

(pause)

Where's the doctor?

SONYA

He's gone.

(pause)

YELENA

Sonya.

SONYA

What?

YELENA

How long are you going to go on being angry with me? We haven't done anything to hurt each other, so why should we be enemies? Enough is enough.

SONYA

I wanted to say it, but . . .

(embraces her)

Let's put it all behind us.

YELENA

That's good.

(both are moved)

SONYA

Has Papa gone to bed?

YELENA

No, he's sitting in the drawing room . . . We don't talk to each other for weeks at a time. God knows why . . .

(seeing the sideboard is open)

What's this?

SONYA

The doctor was having some supper.

YELENA

There's some wine . . . Let's drink to our friendship.

SONYA

Yes, let's.

YELENA

Out of the same glass . . .

(pours it)

It's better that way. So, we are friends?

SONYA

Friends.

(They drink and kiss each other.)

I've been wanting to make peace between us for a long time, but I always felt so ashamed . . .

(She cries.)

YELENA

Why are you crying?

SONYA

It's nothing. Never mind.

YELENA

There, there now.

(cries)

Look at this you've got me crying now, too . . .

(pause)

You're angry with me because you think I married your father for his money . . . If you believe in oaths, I swear to you that I married him for love. I was attracted to him because he was a scholar and a famous man. That wasn't real love, of course. But it felt real at the time. I'm not to blame. But from the very day of our wedding, you haven't stopped punishing me with those piercing, suspicious eyes of yours.

SONYA

It's all right. That's all in the past, so let's forget about it.

YELENA

You shouldn't look at people like that it's so unbecoming. You must believe in people or life will become impossible.

SONYA

Tell me, truthfully, one friend to another. Are you really happy?

YELENA

No.

SONYA

I knew it. One more question, be honest now. Wouldn't you like to have a husband who is young?

YELENA

You're such a little girl. Of course, I would.

(laughs)

Well, ask me something else. Go ahead.

SONYA

Do you like the doctor?

YELENA

Yes, very much.

SONYA

(laughs)

I have a foolish look on my face, haven't I. He's gone, but I can still hear his voice, his footsteps . . . I look at a dark window and see his face in the glass. Let me tell you everything about . . . I can't say it out loud, I feel ashamed . . . Let's go to my room, we can talk there. I look foolish to you, don't I? Tell me . . . Tell me something about him.

YELENA

What should I say?

SONYA

He's a clever man . . . He knows how to do things, he can do anything . . . He heals the sick, he plants trees . . .

YELENA

It's not a question of trees and medicine . . . You see, my dear, he's a man that's blessed with talent. And do you know what being talented means? Courage, freedom of mind and great vision . . . When he plants a tree, he is thinking about what it will be like in a thousand years; he already has a glimpse of man's future happiness. People like him are rare and must be loved . . . He drinks, and sometimes he's a bit coarse, but there's little harm in that. A man of talent in Russia can't remain spotless. Think about the kind of life he leads. Impassable mud roads, freezing weather, snowstorms, vast distances, uncivilized people, poverty and disease at every turn. It would be hard for any man who works and struggles under those conditions to reach the age of forty and remain pure and sober . . .

(kisses her)

I wish you happiness with all my heart. You deserve it.

(rises)

As for me, I'm just a tiresome bore, a minor character . . . In my music, in my husband's house, in my romantic affairs—everything. I have always been a minor character. If you think about it Sonya, I'm a very, very unhappy woman.

(walks about the stage in agitation)

There's no happiness for me in this world. None! Why are you laughing?

SONYA

(laughing, covering her face)

I feel so happy . . . happy!

YELENA

I feel like playing the piano. I'd like to play something right now.

SONYA

Yes, do!

(embraces her)

I can't sleep . . . play something!

YELENA

In a moment. Your father's awake. Music irritates him when he's sick. Go and ask him. If he doesn't mind, I'll play. Go on.

SONYA

I'm going.

(She exits; the sound of the WATCHMAN tapping in the garden)

YELENA

It's been a long time since I've played. I shall play and then . . . cry like a fool.

(through the window)

Yefim, is that you tapping?

WATCHMAN'S VOICE

It's me!

YELENA

Don't tap, the master isn't well.

WATCHMAN'S VOICE

I'll go then.

(whistles for his dogs)

Hey you, Malchik, here boy. Zuchka, good dog. Here Malchik.

(pause)

SONYA

(returning)

He said no!

CURTAIN

ACT III

SCENE: The drawing room of Serebryakov's house. It is night.

AT RISE: VOINITSKY and SOYA are sitting. YELENA is walking around the room thinking about something.

VOINITSKY

Herr Professor has graciously expressed his desire for all of us to meet here in the drawing room by one o'clock.

(looking at his watch)

It is a quarter till. He wants to announce something to the world.

YELENA

Probably business of some sort.

VOINITSKY

He has no business. Unless, of course, you call writing trash, complaining and being jealous business.

SONYA

(reproachfully)

Uncle!

VOINITSKY

All right, I'm sorry. I apologize.

(indicating YELENA)

Would you look at her? With every step she sways from sheer laziness. How charming . . . utterly charming.

YELENA

On and on you go, day in and day out. Don't you get tired of it?

(miserably)

I'm dying of boredom. I don't know what to do.

SONYA

(shrugging her shoulders)

There is plenty to do, if you only want to.

YELENA

For instance?

SONYA

You could help run the estate, teach, treat the sick. There's a lot that needs to be done. When you and Papa weren't here, Uncle Vanya and I used to go the market and sell the flour.

YELENA

I don't know how. Besides, those things don't interest me. It's only in those idealistic novels that people go out to teach and heal the peasants. I can't very well become a teacher or a doctor overnight.

SONYA

What I can't understand is why you don't go out and begin teaching. Give it some time and you'll get used to it.

(embracing her)

Don't be bored, my dear.

(laughing)

I know you can't find anything to do, but boredom and idleness are catching. Look at Uncle Vanya. He does nothing but follow you around like a shadow. And I dropped what I was doing to run in here and talk with you. I've become lazy myself. I can't help it. The doctor only used to visit us on rare occasions, perhaps once a month, and even then it was hard to persuade him. Now he comes here everyday. He's neglecting both his trees and his practice. You seem to have cast a spell over us.

VOINITSKY

Why are you pining away?

(enthusiastically)

Come to your senses, my love. A mermaid's blood runs through your veins, so be a mermaid! Let yourself go for once in your life. Fall madly in love with some water sprite, throw yourself headlong into the deep while Herr Professor and the rest of us look on in amazement.

YELENA

(angrily)

Leave me alone. Your pestering is cruel.
(starting to leave)

VOINITSKY

(preventing her)

One moment, my dear . . . I'm sorry. I apologize.

(kisses her hand)

Peace.

YELENA

It would try the patience of a saint, you know.

VOINITSKY

As a sign of peace I'll bring you a bouquet of roses. I picked them myself, this morning . . . autumn roses, lovely yet sad . . .

(VOINITSKY exits.)

SONYA

Autumn roses, lovely yet sad.

(SONYA and YELENA look out of window.)

YELENA

September already. How will we ever live through the winter here?!

(pause)

Where's the doctor?

SONYA

In Uncle Vanya's room. He's writing something. I'm glad Uncle Vanya left us. I need to talk with you.

YELENA

About what?

SONYA

About what?

(putting her head on YELENA's breast)

YELENA

There, there, now.

(strokes SONYA's hair)

It's all right.

SONYA

I'm not pretty.

YELENA

You have beautiful hair.

SONYA

No!

(turning to look at herself in the mirror)

No! When a woman isn't pretty people always say, "You have beautiful eyes, you have beautiful hair . . . " I've loved him for six years, loved him more than my own mother. I'm always hearing his voice or feeling the touch of his hand. I look at the door and wait, thinking he'll walk in at any moment. And I keep running to you to talk about him. Now he's here everyday, but he doesn't look at me, he doesn't see me . . . My heart is on fire and I have no hope. None. None at all.

(desperately)

Oh, God . . . I pray all night long . . . I often walk up to him, start talking and look into his eyes. I have no pride left or even the strength to control myself. Yesterday, I confessed everything to Uncle Vanya . . . All the servants know I love him. Everyone knows.

YELENA

Does he?

SONYA

No. He doesn't notice me.

YELENA

(thoughtfully)

He's a strange man . . . I'll tell you what. Let me have a talk with him. I'll be very subtle—nothing direct—just a hint.

(pause)

Really. How much longer can you stand not knowing? Will you let me?

(SONYA nods her head.)

Good. Does he love you or not? That shouldn't be hard to find out. Now, don't be embarrassed, my dear. There's nothing to worry about. I'll be so discreet, he won't even notice. We just need to know whether it is yes or no.

(pause)

If it is no, he'd better stop coming here, don't you think?

(SONYA nods her head.)

It would be easier if you didn't see him. We won't put it off any longer. We'll begin cross-examining him right away. He wanted to show me some charts he's been preparing. Go tell him I want to see him.

SONYA

(very upset)

You will tell me the whole truth?

YELENA

Yes, of course. The truth, no matter what it is, can never be as dreadful as not knowing. Trust me.

SONYA

Yes, yes. I'll tell him you wish to see his charts.

(starting to leave and stops by the door)

Not knowing is better . . . at least there is hope.

YELENA

I beg your pardon?

SONYA

Nothing.

(SONYA exits.)

YELENA

(alone)

There's nothing worse than knowing someone else's secret and not being able to help.

(thoughtfully)

He's not in love with her, that's clear. But why shouldn't he marry her? True, she isn't pretty, but for a country doctor at his age, she'd make a perfect wife. She's intelligent, kind, pure . . .

(pause)

But that's not the point. I know what the poor girl is going through. In the middle of this desperate boredom where all the people are pale grey shadows drifting from room to room, where the talk is trivial and vulgar, where people only eat, drink and sleep, he appears from time to time. He's different from the rest—handsome, interesting, fascinating like a bright moon rising in the darkness. To fall under his spell and forget everything . . . I think I am affected by him, too. When he isn't here, I'm bored, and now, I find myself smiling at the thought of him. Uncle Vanya says I have a mermaid's blood in my veins. "Let yourself go for once in your life." Maybe I should . . . Fly away, free as a bird, away from all of you, from your sleepy faces, from your trivial talk, to forget all of you even exist. But I'm a coward, too shy . . . My conscience would torment me . . . He comes here everyday now, and I can guess why. I already feel guilty, Sonya. I want to fall on my knees, crying, begging you to forgive me . . .

(ASTROV enters with a chart.)

ASTROV

Good afternoon.

(shaking her hand)

You wanted to see my drawings?

YELENA

You promised yesterday to show me your work. Are you free?

ASTROV

Of course.

(He spreads the chart out on the card
table and fastens it down with
thumb- tacks.)

Where were you born?

YELENA

(helping him)

St. Petersburg.

ASTROV

And where did you study?

YELENA

At the Conservatory of Music.

ASTROV

This probably won't interest you.

YELENA

Why? I might not be familiar with the countryside, but I've read a lot.

ASTROV

I have my own worktable in Vanya's room. When I am beyond tired to the point of exhaustion, I drop everything, run over here, and amuse myself for an hour or two with this stuff . . . Vanya and Sonya are clicking away on the abacus, and I sit nearby at my table, drawing and painting. It's warm and peaceful, and the cricket chirps. But I don't allow myself this pleasure very often, maybe once a month.

(pointing to the chart)

Now, look here. This shows our part of the country as it was fifty years ago. The light and dark green colors represent the forests. Half of the entire area was covered by forests. The red cross- hatching over the green was the home of elk and wild goats. Both flora and fauna are shown here. On this lake there were swans, geese, ducks and birds of all kinds. Like the old folks used to say, "a power" of birds. They used to blacken the sky. Beside the villages you can see scattered settlements, small farms, monasteries, water mills . . . a lot of cattle and horses. They're shown in blue. In this district, for instance, the blue was thick. There were herds of horses here and here with two or three on every farm.

(pause)

Now look down here. This is twenty-five years ago. Only a third of the area is covered with forests. There are still some elk, but the goats are gone. The green and blue colors have become paler. And so on and so on. Now, lets move to this section, our district as it is today. The green color here and there exist in patches rather than solid areas. The elk, swans and wood grouse have vanished. The old villages, farms, monasteries and water mills have disappeared without a trace. In general, it's a sad picture of gradual decay that should be complete in another ten or fifteen years. You will say there are cultural influences at work here, that the old ways of life must give way to the new. Yes, I could understand it if the forests were destroyed to make room for new roads and railroads, to build factories and schools. The peasants would become healthier, more educated and better off. But, as you can see, nothing has been done! We still have the same swamps and mosquitoes, a lack of roads, poverty, typhus, diphtheria and fires . . . What we have before us is decay resulting from a desperate struggle for existence. People don't have the strength, they're backward and ignorant. And because they are cold, hungry and ill they will instinctively grasp for the quick solution. Anything to satisfy their hunger, to warm themselves, and in so doing, they destroy everything around them without a thought for the future. Nearly everything has been destroyed already, but nothing has been created to take its place.

(coldly)

I see from your expression this doesn't interest you.

YELENA

But I understand so little about it.

ASTROV

There's nothing to understand. You're just not interested.

YELENA

To be honest, my thoughts were somewhere else. Forgive me. I must put you through a little cross-examination, and I feel embarrassed about it. I don't know quite where to begin.

ASTROV

A cross-examination?

YELENA

A cross-examination, yes, but a harmless one. Let's sit down.

(They sit.)

This concerns a certain young person. Let's be honest with one another, like friends open and to the point. We'll talk, and then everything will be forgotten. All right?

ASTROV

All right.

YELENA

This concerns my stepdaughter, Sonya. What are your feelings toward her?

ASTROV

I respect her.

YELENA

Do you like her as a woman?

ASTROV

(after a pause)

No.

YELENA

Two or three more words and we'll be done. You haven't noticed anything, then?

ASTROV

No.

YELENA

(taking his hand)

You don't love her; I can see it in your eyes. She is in a lot of pain. You must realize that and . . . stop coming here.

ASTROV

(rising)

My time has already past . . . Besides, I have no time for such . . .

(shrugging his shoulders)

When would I have time?

(He is embarrassed.)

YELENA

Ugh! What an unpleasant conversation. I'm so upset. I feel as though I've been dragging a two-ton weight around. Anyway, thank goodness it's over. Let's forget this discussion ever took place and . . . and just go away. You're an intelligent man, you understand . . .

(pause)

Oh, my. I'm afraid I'm blushing.

ASTROV

If you had told me this a month or two ago, perhaps I would have considered it, but now . . .

(shrugging his shoulders)

Still, if I'm causing her pain, then of course . . . There's one thing I don't understand, though. Why was this cross-examination neces- sary?

(He looks into her eyes and wags his finger.)

Aren't you the sly one!

YELENA

What do you mean?

ASTROV

(laughs)

Sly indeed. All right, Sonya may find all this painful, I won't argue with that. But why this cross-examination?

(quickly, preventing her from speaking)

Don't act so surprised, you know perfectly well why I've been coming here everyday . . . why I come and who I want to see. I'm weak, and you know that all too well, my beautiful bird of prey.

YELENA

Bird of prey? I don't know what you mean.

ASTROV

You hunger for a victim. I've done nothing for an entire month. I've dropped everything just so I could be near you and that pleases you no end. Well, then. I am conquered. I'm sure you knew that without all the questions.

(folds his arms and bows his head)

Swoop down, beautiful bird, and carry me away.

YELENA

Are you out of your mind?

ASTROV

(laughing)

Are you shy . . .

YELENA

I'm not that kind of person. I'm far better than that. I swear it.

(She tries to go but he bars her way.)

ASTROV

I'm leaving today, and I won't be coming back . . .

(taking her by the arm, looking around)

Where can we see each other? Tell me quickly. Where? Someone might come in. Quickly, while there is still time.

(passionately)

You're incredible . . . one kiss . . .

YELENA

I swear to you

ASTROV

(stopping her from speaking)

Why? There's no need to swear . . . no need for words. So lovely . . . Such pretty hands.

(kisses her hand)

YELENA

That's enough, now. Go away.

(pulling her hand away)

You're forgetting yourself.

ASTROV

Tell me, Yelena, where can we meet tomorrow?

(taking her by the waist)

You see. It's inevitable. We must see each other.

(He kisses her. As he does, VOINITSKY enters with a bouquet of roses and stops in the doorway.)

YELENA

(not seeing VOINITSKY)

Take pity on me.

ASTROV

No.

YELENA

(laying her head against ASTROV's chest)

No.

(She moves to go and ASTROV holds her by the waist.)

ASTROV

Come to the forest tomorrow . . . around two o'clock . . . All right? Hm? You'll come?

YELENA

(seeing VOINITSKY)

Let me go!

(moving away toward the window, very embarrassed)

This is terrible.

(VOINITSKY places the bouquet of flowers down on the chair; very upset, he wipes his face and neck with a handkerchief.)

VOINITSKY

Never mind . . . it's nothing . . . never mind . . .

ASTROV

(inwardly angry)

Today, my good friend, the weather is not too bad. It was cloudy this morning. Looked like rain but now the sun is shining. I have to admit this has been a splendid autumn . . . and the winter crops are doing well.

(rolling up chart)

There's just one thing—the days are growing shorter . . .

(ASTROV exits.)

YELENA

(quickly moving to VOINITSKY)

You must try you best, use all you influence, to see that my husband and I leave this place today. Do you hear? Today!

VOINITSKY

(wiping his face)

What? Oh, yes . . . uh . . . I saw what happened, Yelena, I saw it all . . .

(SEREBRYAKOV, SONYA TELEGIN and MARINA enter.)

TELEGIN

You know, Professor, I've been feeling poorly myself these last couple of days. It's my head; it's been . . .

SEREBRYAKOV

Where are the others? I hate this house it's like a labyrinth. Twenty-six enormous rooms, people wander off so you can never find anyone.

(rings)

Ask Maria Vasilyevna and Yelena Andreevna to come in here.

YELENA

I'm here.

SEREBRYAKOV

Ladies and gentlemen, please sit down.

SONYA

(moving to YELENA, impatiently)

What did he say?

YELENA

I'll tell you later.

SONYA

You're trembling. Something's upset you.

(studying her face)

I understand . . . He said he wouldn't be coming anymore . . . Right? Tell me. Is that what he said?

(YELENA nods.)

SEREBRYAKOV

(to TELEGIN)

You can learn to live with bad health if you put your mind to it. But the thing I can't endure is this way of life in the country. I feel like I'm living on another planet. Sit down, ladies and gentlemen, please. Sonya!

(She does not hear him.)

Sonya?

(pause)

She's gone deaf.

(to MARINA)

Nanny, you sit, too.

(MARINA sits down and begins knitting a stocking.)

Ladies and gentlemen, hang your ears, as they say, on the hook of attention.

(laughs)

VOINITSKY

(very upset)

I doubt if I'm needed here. May I go?

SEREBRYAKOV

No, you are needed here more than anyone else.

VOINITSKY

What do you want from me?

SEREBRYAKOV

Want from you? Why are you so upset?

(pause)
If I've offended you in some way, please forgive me.

VOINITSKY
Don't use that tone of voice with me. Let's get on with it . . . What do you want?

(MARIA VASILYEVNA enters.)

SEREBRYAKOV
Here is Maman. I'll begin, then.

(pause)
I've invited you here, ladies and gentlemen, to announce that the Inspector General is on his way.

(pause)
All joking aside, this is a serious matter. I have called all of you together to ask for your help and advice, and knowing your customary kindness, I hope to receive it. I am a scholar, a man of books, and unfamiliar with the practical aspects of life. I could not manage without the assistance of experienced people, so I look to your guidance, Ivan Petrovich, and you too, Ilya Ilyich, and you, Maman . . . The point is, "manet omnes una nox", meaning no one lives forever. I'm old and I'm failing, so I think it's time to set my affairs in order concerning my property insofar as they affect my family. My life is over so I'm not thinking about myself. But I do have a young wife and an unmarried daughter.

(pause)
It is not possible for me to go on living here in the country. We're just not made for this kind of life. And the income from the estate is not enough to support our living in town. If the forest was sold, for example, that would be an extreme measure, and it would soon be exhausted. What we need is a way to guarantee a permanent, more or less definite income figure. I have devised a means to accomplish it, and I have the honor to propose it for your consideration. I won't bore you with details but rather explain it in general terms. On average, our estate yields a maximum of two per cent. I propose to sell it. If we invest the proceeds in securities, we should receive four or five per cent. And I think there will be a surplus of several thousand rubles—enough to purchase a small country cottage in Finland.

VOINITSKY

Wait . . . I can't believe what I'm hearing. Say it again.

SEREBRYAKOV

Invest the money in securities and use the surplus to purchase a country cottage in Finland.

VOINITSKY

Not about a cottage . . . you said something else.

SEREBRYAKOV

I propose to sell the estate.

VOINITSKY

That's it. You're going to sell the estate. What a brilliant idea! And what do you have in store for my aging mother and me? And what about Sonya? What about us?

SEREBRYAKOV

We will discuss it all at the proper time. Not now.

VOINITSKY

Just a moment. It looks as though I have been a complete fool. Up until now, I was stupid enough to believe that this estate belonged to Sonya. My late father bought this estate as a dowry for my sister. Up till now, I was naive enough to believe that the estate passed from my sister to Sonya. I had no idea we were living under Turkish law!

SEREBRYAKOV

Yes, the estate belongs to Sonya. No one's disputing that. Without Sonya's consent, I would never think of selling it. But after all, this is for Sonya's benefit.

VOINITSKY

This is unbelievable, unbelievable! Either I'm losing my mind or . . . or . . .

MARIA VASILYEVNA

(to VOINITSKY)

Jean, don't argue with Alexandre. He knows right from wrong much better than any of us.

VOINITSKY

No, give me some water.

(drinks)

Go on. Say whatever you like.

SEREBRYAKOV

I don't understand why you are so disturbed. If everyone finds it unsuitable, I won't insist.

(pause)

TELEGIN

(embarrassed)

I have a very deep respect for scholarship, your Excellency, and also for family feelings. My brother, Gregory Ilyich, his wife's brother—perhaps you know him—Konstantin Trofimovich Lakedemodov. He held a Master of Arts.

VOINITSKY

Not now, Waffles. We're talking business here . . . later on, all right?

(to SEREBRYAKOV)

Here, ask him. The estate was bought from his uncle.

SEREBRYAKOV

Why? What purpose would that serve?

VOINITSKY

This estate was purchased, at that time, for ninety-five thousand rubles. Father paid seventy thousand which left a mortgage of twenty-five thousand rubles. Now listen . . . This estate would never have been purchased in the first place if I hadn't given up my inheritance in favor of my sister, whom I loved dearly. What's more, I worked like an ox for ten years to pay off the entire mortgage.

SEREBRYAKOV

I'm sorry I brought the whole thing up.

VOINITSKY

This estate is free of debt and in operating condition only because of my own personal efforts. And now I'm getting on in years, I'm to be picked up by the scruff of the neck and thrown off.

SEREBRYAKOV

I don't understand what you're driving at.

VOINITSKY

For twenty-five years I've managed this estate. I've labored and sent you the money like the most conscientious of stewards . . . and you never bothered to thank me once. All this time you paid me a pauper's wage of five hundred rubles a year, and not once did it cross your mind to pay me one ruble more.

SEREBRYAKOV

How was I to know? I'm not a practical man. I don't understand these things. You could have given yourself more, as much as you would have liked.

VOINITSKY

To have stolen, you mean? You ridicule me now because I didn't steal? It would have been justifiable; at least I wouldn't be a pauper now.

MARIA VASILYEVNA

(sternly)

Jean!

TELEGIN

(very upset)

Vanya, my friend, don't do this . . . I'm trembling . . . don't spoil good relations.

(kisses him)

Don't do it.

VOINITSKY

For twenty-five years I've been living like a mole, buried inside these four walls with this mother of mine . . . All our thoughts and feelings were centered around you. During the day we talked about you and your work. We were so proud of you; we practically worshipped your very name. Our nights were wasted reading books and journals that I have come to despise with all my being.

TELEGIN

Don't, Vanya. Please . . . I can't take it.

SEREBRYAKOV

(angrily)

I don't understand what is it you want?

VOINITSKY

We thought of you as a superior being. We knew your articles, word for word. But now my eyes have been opened, and I can see everything clearly for the first time. You write about art but you understand nothing about it. All your works, which I used to adore, aren't worth the paper they're written on. You've really pulled the wool over our eyes.

SEREBRYAKOV

Enough! Would someone please reason with him. I'm leaving.

YELENA

(to VOINITSKY)

Ivan Petrovich, I demand you stop this immediately. Do you hear me?

VOINITSKY

I won't stop it.

(blocking SEREBRYAKOV's way)

Wait I'm not finished! You have ruined my life! I haven't lived. I've been robbed of the best years of my life, and you're the thief who took them from me. You are my worst enemy!

TELEGIN

I can't stand this . . . I can't . . . I'm leaving.

(He exits in great distress.)

SEREBRYAKOV

What do you want? And how dare you speak to me like that? You're nothing, a nobody. If this estate is yours, then take it! I don't need it!

YELENA

I'm not staying a moment longer in this living hell.

(screaming)

I can't take it!!

VOINITSKY

My life has been wasted. I have talent, intelligence, courage . . . If I had lived a normal life, I could have been a Schopenhauer or a Dostoevski . . . What am I saying? I must be losing my mind . . . Mother, oh . . . please help me.

MARIA VASILYEVNA

(sternly)

Do as Alexandre says.

SONYA

(kneels in front of MARINA and presses close to her)

Nanny!

VOINITSKY

Mother! What am I to do? No, don't tell me. I know what to do now.

(to SEREBRYAKOV)

I'll do something you'll never forget.

(VOINITSKY exits; MARIA VASILYEVNA follows.)

SEREBRYAKOV

Ladies and gentlemen, would someone please tell me what this is all about? And keep that madman away from me! How can I be expected to live under the same roof with him? His room is almost next to mine. Make him move into the village or one of the cottages on the estate . . . or I will move out . . . But I can't stay in the same house with him . . .

YELENA

(to her husband)

We'll leave this place today. Make the arrangements at once.

SEREBRYAKOV

The man's a nobody.

SONYA

(tearfully)

Please, Papa, try to understand. Uncle Vanya and I are so unhappy.

(controlling herself)

Try to understand. Remember when you were younger, Uncle Vanya and Grandmother used to spend their evenings translating books for you, copying papers . . . Night after night! Uncle Vanya and I have worked without rest, afraid to spend anything on ourselves because we were sending everything to you. We earned our daily bread. I'm not saying it right, it's coming out all wrong but . . . you've got to try to understand, Papa. Show some compassion.

YELENA

(to her husband, upset)

For God's sake, Alexandre, talk it out with him. Please!

SEREBRYAKOV

All right. I'll talk with him. I'm not blaming him for anything. I'm not angry, but you have got to agree with me that his behavior is bizarre. All right, then. I'll go see him.

(SEREBRYAKOV exits.)

YELENA

Be gentle with him; try to calm him down.

(YELENA exits following SEREBRYAKOV.)

SONYA

Nanny . . .

MARINA

Never mind, child, never you mind. The geese will cackle, and then they stop. Cackle and stop.

SONYA

Nanny!

MARINA

(stroking her hair)

You're shivering like you've been out in the freezing cold! There, there, my little orphan. God is merciful. Some lime flower tea—or raspberry—and you'll feel much better. Don't grieve, little orphan.

(looking at the door, angrily)

No more cackling, the geese are in their nests.

(A shot is heard offstage. YELENA's scream is heard. SONYA shudders.)

Damn!

SEREBRYAKOV

(running on, reeling with fright)

Stop him! Someone stop him! He's gone mad!

(YELENA and VOINITSKY struggle in the doorway.)

YELENA

(trying to take the revolver from him)

Give it to me! Give it to me, I tell you!

VOINITSKY

Let me go, Yelena! Let me go!

(Freeing himself, he runs in looking for SEREBRYAKOV.)

Where is he? Ah, there he is!

(fires at him)

Bang!

(pause)

Missed him? Again? Oh, God!

(He drops to the floor in front of a chair and beats his fist against the floor.)

Damn, damn, damn, damn . . .

(SEREBRYAKOV is stunned. YELENA leans against the wall looking faint.)

YELENA

Take me away from here. Take me away, kill me, anything! I can't stay here, I can't.

VOINITSKY

(in despair)

Oh, what am I doing? What am I doing?

SONYA

(quietly)

Nanny.

CURTAIN

ACT IV

SCENE: Voinitsky's room which serves as his bedroom and the estate office. By the window is a large table with account books and papers of all kinds; also a desk, cupboards and scales. There is a smaller table for ASTROV with paints and drawing materials and beside it is a portfolio. A bird cage with a starling in it. On the wall is a map of Africa which has no particular function. A huge sofa upholstered in oil cloth. On the left a door leads to the other rooms of the house; on the right a door to the porch. On the floor, in front of the right door, is a mat so peasants won't dirty the floor. An autumn evening and very still.

AT RISE: TELEGIN and MARINA sit facing each other, winding wool.

TELEGIN

Hurry up or they'll be calling us to say goodbye. They've already ordered the horses brought around.

MARINA

(trying to wind faster)

Just a little bit left.

TELEGIN

They're traveling to Kharkov . . . going to live there.

MARINA

It's for the best.

TELEGIN

They had quite a fright . . . Yelena Andreevna says, "I won't stay here another hour . . . we're going and that's final. We'll go to Kharkov," she says, "and after we've had a look around we'll send for our things." They're leaving with only the clothes on their backs. Isn't that something? They were destined to live elsewhere . . . that's what it is . . . it's fate.

MARINA

It's for the best. All that ruckus and the shooting, why it's shameful!

TELEGIN

Yes. It was a scene worthy of a painter's brush.

MARINA

I wish my eyes had never seen it.

(pause)

We can go back to the old ways now, live like we did before. Morning tea at eight, dinner at noon and supper in the evening. Everything at its proper time, like other good Christians.

(with a sigh)

It's been a long time since an old sinner like me has tasted noodles.

TELEGIN

That's right. They haven't cooked noodles for quite a while now.

(pause)

Quite a while . . . This morning I was walking through the village, and a shopkeeper shouted after me, "Hey, you leech, how does it feel to live off others?" It made me feel so bitter.

MARINA

Don't pay any attention to him, my dear. We're all leeches when you think about it . . . living off the grace of God. You, Sonya, Ivan Petrovich, no one sits around doing nothing, we all keep working! All of us . . . Where is Sonya?

TELEGIN

In the garden. She and the doctor are looking for Ivan Petrovich. They're afraid he might lay hands on himself.

MARINA

Where is his pistol?

TELEGIN

(whispering)

I hid it in the cellar!

MARINA

(with a smile)

Sinful! What goings on!

(VOINITSKY and ASTROV enter from outside.)

VOINITSKY

Leave me alone.

(to MARINA and TELEGIN)

Go away. Can't you leave me alone for a single hour? I can't stand being watched.

TELEGIN

Of course, Vanya.

(He tiptoes out the door.)

MARINA

You old gander. Ga, ga, ga!

(She gathers her wool and exits.)

VOINITSKY

Leave me alone!

ASTROV

With the greatest of pleasure. I should have left here long ago, but I'll say it again. I'm not leaving until you give back what you took from me.

VOINITSKY

I haven't taken anything from you.

ASTROV

I'm serious. Don't make me wait. I should have left hours ago.

VOINITSKY

I haven't taken anything, I tell you.

(both sit)

ASTROV

Oh? All right, I'll wait a little longer . . . but then, I'm afraid, I will have to use force. We'll tie you up and search you. I mean it.

VOINITSKY

If that's what you want.

(pause)

I'm such a fool. Imagine shooting twice and missing both times! I'll never be able to forgive myself.

ASTROV

If you had to shoot somebody, why didn't you just put the gun to your own head and pull the trigger?

VOINITSKY

Strange, isn't it? I tried to murder a man, but I'm not under arrest. I'm not even charged with anything. They must think I'm insane. But other people who disguise their utter lack of talent, mediocrity and heartlessness behind the mask of a professor, a master of knowledge, they're not. Neither are women who marry old men and then openly deceive them. I saw you, I saw her in your arms!

ASTROV

That's right and as far as I'm concerned you can go straight to hell!

VOINITSKY

(looking at the door)

The earth itself is insane if it still holds the like of you.

ASTROV

Now, that's a stupid thing to say.

VOINITSKY

Of course it is. I'm insane; I'm not responsible. So, I have a right to say stupid things.

ASTROV

Your act is getting old. You're not insane, you're just eccentric . . . an oddball. There used to be a time when I believed every oddball was sick, abnormal. Now, I've come to the conclusion that eccentricity is man's normal state. You are perfectly normal.

VOINITSKY

(covers face with his hands)

I'm so ashamed! If you only knew how ashamed I feel.

(in despair)

It's so ungodly painful I can't stand it.

(leaning down over the table)

What am I to do? What am I to do?

ASTROV

Nothing.

VOINITSKY

Give me something to take! Oh my God . . . I'm forty-seven years old. What if I live to be sixty? I'll have another thirteen years to go. That's a long time. How can I fill up thirteen years. What will I be doing? Can you imagine . . .

(squeezing ASTROV's hand)

Can you imagine what it would be like if you could live the rest of your life in some new way? If you could just wake up some clear, quiet morning and feel you're beginning a fresh new life, that your past is forgotten like a wisp of smoke vanishing into the air.

(crying)

To begin again . . . tell me how to begin . . . where to start?

ASTROV

(annoyed)

Come on, now! What do you mean a new life. Our situation, yours and mine, is hopeless.

VOINITSKY

It is?

ASTROV

I'm sure of it.

VOINITSKY

Give me something.

(indicating his heart)

I'm burning in here.

ASTROV

(shouting angrily)

Stop it!

(more gently)

Those people who come after us, in another century or two, who will despise us for leading such stupid and wasteful lives, maybe they'll find a way to be happy. But you and I, there's only one hope for us—the hope that as we lie in our graves, we'll have peaceful dreams.

(sighs)

Yes, my good friend. In the entire district there were only two decent, cultured men, you and I. But ten years of this wretched provincial existence has dragged us down. Its rotten atmosphere has poisoned our blood and made us as petty and vulgar as everyone else.

(with more energy)

But you're not going to talk your way out of this. You give me back what you took.

VOINITSKY

I didn't take anything.

ASTROV

You took a small bottle of morphine from my medical bag. Listen, if you really intend to end it all, go into the woods and shoot yourself. But give me back the morphine or people will start talking. They'll believe I gave it to you . . . It's going to be bad enough conducting the postmortem. Do you think I would enjoy that?

(SONYA enters.)

VOINITSKY

Leave me alone.

ASTROV

(to SONYA)

Your uncle has taken a small bottle of morphine from my medical bag, and he won't give it back. Would you tell him, please, that it's . . . not a clever thing to do. Besides, I'm wasting my time. I need to be on my way.

SONYA

Uncle Vanya, did you take the morphine?

(pause)

ASTROV

He took it. I know he did.

SONYA

Give it back. Why do you want to frighten us?

(tenderly)

Give it back, Uncle Vanya. I'm probably as unhappy as you, but I'm not going to give in to despair. I'm bearing it, and I will continue to bear it until my life comes to a natural end. You must bear it as well.

(pause)

Give it back.

(kisses his hand)

My dearest Uncle, please. Give it back.

(cries)

You're a kind man, a good man. You'll do it for us, won't you? You must bear it, Uncle. Please.

(VOINITSKY gets the bottle from the desk and gives it to ASTROV.)

VOINITSKY

Here, take it.

(to SONYA)

We must get to work right away. We have to start doing something or else I can't go on.

SONYA

Yes, yes, work. As soon as we see them all off, we'll get down to work.

(nervously sorting through papers at the table)

We've let everything go.

ASTROV

(puts bottle into his bag and tightens the straps)

Now I can be on my way.

(YELENA enters.)

YELENA

Ivan Petrovich, are you here? We're leaving now . . . Go to see Alexandre he has something he wants to say to you.

SONYA

Go on, Uncle Vanya.

(taking him by the arm)

I'll go with you. You and Papa must make peace once and for all. You simply must.

(SONYA and VOINITSKY exit.)

YELENA

I'm leaving.

(extending her hand to him)

Goodbye.

ASTROV

Already.

YELENA

They've brought the horses.

ASTROV

Goodbye.

YELENA

Today you promised me you would go away from here.

ASTROV

I know. I'm leaving in a moment.

(pause)

You're frightened?

(taking her hand)

Is it really so bad?

YELENA

Yes.

ASTROV

Perhaps you should stay. What do you think . . . We could meet tomorrow in the forest . . .

YELENA

No . . . the decision has already been made . . . You see, that's how I have the courage to face you because the decision has been made that we're leaving. There is something I would ask you. Think of me as a better person. I would like you to respect me.

ASTROV

Oh . . .

(making a gesture of impatience)

Please, stay on here. You have to face the fact that you have nothing in the world to do, no purpose in life, nothing to occupy your mind, and sooner or later you're going to give in to your feelings. It's inevitable. But not somewhere like Kharkov or Kursk. Better here, in the lap of nature itself . . . at least it has a poetic quality, beautiful autumns . . . there is a forest and the ruins of old country houses like those described by Turgenev.

YELENA

You're a funny man . . . I'm angry with you but . . . I will remember you with pleasure. You are one of a kind, original and unique. We'll never see each other again so why hide it? I was a bit in love with you, but . . . Well, let's just shake hands and say goodbye as friends. Remember me kindly.

ASTROV

(shaking her hand)

Yes, you'd better go . . .

(thoughtfully)

You seem to be a good, sincere person but you have a peculiar disposition. Before you came here, everyone was working, building, creating . . . But the moment you and your husband arrived, we dropped everything and spent the summer attending you and your husband's gout. Both of you infected us with your idleness. I became infatuated with you and have done nothing for an entire month. And all during this time, people have been getting sick and peasants have been grazing their cattle in my newly planted forest. So, there it is. You wreak havoc wherever you go. I'm joking, of course, but nevertheless, it is . . . strange. In fact, if you had stayed I'm quite certain the devastation would have been enormous— probably the end for me and not much better for you. So, you'd best be going. Finita la commedia!

YELENA

(She takes a pencil from his table and quickly hides it.)

I'm taking this to remember you by.

ASTROV

It's a curious thing, isn't it . . . We've come to know each other and now, for some reason . . . we'll never see each other again. It's the way of the world, I suppose . . . Before anyone comes in, before Uncle Vanya walks in with a bouquet, would you let me . . . kiss you . . . goodbye?

(kisses her cheek)

There . . . It's done.

YELENA

I wish you the best.

(looking around)

Oh, for once in my life . . .

(She embraces him suddenly and then both move quickly away from each other.)

I must go.

ASTROV

Go quickly. If the horses are ready, you can be on your way.

YELENA

I think they are coming.

(Both listen.)

ASTROV

Finita!

(SEREBRYAKOV, VOINITSKY, MARIA ASILYEVNA, carrying a book; TELEGIN and SONYA enter.)

SEREBRYAKOV

Let bygones be bygones. After all that has happened, I've been through so much and thought about so many things, I think I could write a treatise on how we should live our lives, for posterity's sake. I gladly accept your apologies and beg you to accept mine as well. Goodbye.

VOINITSKY

You will receive exactly the same amount as you did before. Everything will be as it was.

(YELENA embraces SONYA.)

SEREBRYAKOV

(kissing MARIA VASILYEVNA's hand)

Maman . . .

MARIA VASILYEVNA

(kissing SEREBRYAKOV)

Alexandre, have your picture taken again and send it to me. You know how much you mean to me.

TELEGIN

Goodbye, your Excellency. Don't forget us.

SEREBRYAKOV

(kissing his daughter)

Goodbye, my dear. Goodbye everyone.

(to ASTROV)

Thank you for the pleasure of your company. I want you to know I respect your way of thinking, your impulsiveness and enthusiasm, but let an old man voice an observation in his farewell remarks. Ladies and gentlemen, you must get to work. Something useful must be done.

(bows to all in general)

I wish you all the best.

(SEREBRYAKOV exits followed by MARIA VASILYEVNA and SONYA.)

VOINITSKY

(kisses YELENA's hand)

Goodbye . . . Forgive me . . . We will never see each other again.

YELENA

(moved)

Goodbye, my dear.

(kisses him on the head and exits)

ASTROV

(to TELEGIN)

Waffles, you may as well tell them to bring my horses around at the same time.

TELEGIN

Of course.

(TELEGIN exits. ASTROV and VOINITSKY are left alone.)

ASTROV

(clearing paints from the table and putting them in a suitcase)

Why don't you go see them off?

VOINITSKY

Let them go. I . . . can't. I feel so depressed. I've got to find something to do. Quickly. Work, that's it. Work.

(He rummages through papers on the table. Pause. Harness bells are heard.)

ASTROV

They've gone. No doubt the professor is glad. I have a feeling he'll never return.

MARINA

(entering)

They've gone.

(She sits in an armchair and knits her stocking.)

SONYA

(entering)

They've gone.

(wiping her eyes)

May God protect them.

(to her uncle)

Let's do something, Uncle Vanya.

VOINITSKY

Work. We must get to work.

SONYA

It's been a long, long time since we sat down together at this table.

(lights lamp on table)

There doesn't seem to be any ink.

(carries inkwell to the cupboard and fills it)

I feel sad now they've gone.

(MARIA VASILYEVNA enters slowly.)

MARIA VASILYEVNA

They've gone.

(sits and begins reading)

SONYA

(sits at the table and pages through an account book)

Uncle Vanya, let's begin by settling the accounts. We're awfully far behind. Someone else sent us a second notice for their account today. You do one and I'll do another.

VOINITSKY

(writing)

To the account of Mr. . . .

(They both sit and write.)

MARINA

(yawning)

I'm ready for bed.

ASTROV

It's quiet . . . pens scratching, a cricket chirping . . . warm and cozy. I don't feel like leaving.

(Harness bells are heard.)

Ah, they're bringing my horses. It seems the only thing that remains is to say goodbye to you, my friends, and goodbye to my table, and then be on my way.

(places maps in the portfolio)

MARINA

Why are you in such a hurry to leave. Stay here for a while.

ASTROV

I can't.

VOINITSKY

(writing)

. . . there remains a debt in the amount of two rubles and seventy-five kopecks . . .

(A WORKMAN enters.)

WORKMAN

(to ASTROV)

Your horses are ready.

ASTROV

Yes, I heard.

(handing him the medical bag, suitcase and portfolio)

Here, take these things. Make sure you don't crush the portfolio.

WORKMAN

Yes, sir.

(He exits.)

ASTROV

Well . . .

(He starts saying his goodbyes.)

SONYA

When will we see you again?

ASTROV

Not before next summer, I imagine. Hardly in the winter . . . Unless, of course, something happens, then I'll be here.

(shaking her hand)

Thank you for your kindness, your hospitality and . . . well. . . thank you for everything.

(He moves to Nanny and kisses her on the head.)

Goodbye my old one.

MARINA

You're not leaving without some tea are you?

ASTROV

I don't care for any, Nanny.

MARINA

A little vodka, maybe?

ASTROV

(indecisively)

Oh . . . maybe.

(MARINA exits. Pause.)

My trace horse has come down lame for some reason. I noticed it yesterday when Petrushka was leading him to water.

VOINITSKY

You'll need to have him reshod.

ASTROV

Yes, I'll have to see the blacksmith in the village. Nothing else can be done about it.

(He moves to the map of Africa and looks at it.)

I suppose the heat in Africa must be pretty intense about now.

VOINITSKY

You're probably right.

(MARINA enters with a glass of vodka and a piece of bread on tray.)

MARINA

Here you are.

(as he drinks the vodka)

To your good health, my dear.

(bows low)

Have a little bread with it.

ASTROV

No, this is enough . . . and I wish all of you the best.

(to MARINA)

Sit down, Nanny. I'll see myself out.

(ASTROV exits followed by SONYA who carries a candle to show him out. MARINA sits in her own armchair.)

VOINITSKY

(writing)

February the second, vegetable oil, twenty pounds . . . February the sixteenth, more vegetable oil, twenty pounds . . . Buckwheat . . .

(Pause. Harness bells are heard.)

MARINA

He's gone.

(Pause. SONYA enters and returns candle to the table.)

SONYA

He's gone.

VOINITSKY

(calculates on abacus and writes)

Total . . . fifteen . . . twenty-five . . .

(SONYA sits and writes.)

MARINA

(yawns)

Goodness gracious me.

(TELEGIN enters on tiptoe, sits by the door and quietly tunes his guitar. VOINITSKY strokes SONYA's hair.)

VOINITSKY

My dear one. I am feeling so low. If you only knew the depth of my despair.

SONYA

What can we do? We have to go on living

(pause)

We'll go on living, Uncle Vanya. We'll live through a long series of days and endless evenings. We'll patiently bear whatever Fate has in store for us. We'll work for others from now into our old age, without ever finding rest. And when our time comes, we'll die humbly; and there, beyond the grave, we will say that we suffered and cried and had a bitter life . . . and God will take pity on us. And you and I, my dear Uncle Vanya, we shall see a life that is bright, beautiful and good. We'll rejoice and look back on our present life with tenderness and smile . . . and we will find peace. We will, Uncle, I believe it with all my heart.

(She kneels before him and lays her head in her hands. In a in a weary voice she speaks.)

We shall rest.

(TELEGIN quietly plays his guitar.)

We shall rest. We'll hear the angels and see the sky sparkling with diamonds. We'll see all the world's evil and all our own suffering drown in the mercy that will flood the whole world. Our life will become quiet and gentle and as sweet as a caress. I believe it, I believe it . . .

(wiping away tears with his handkerchief)

Poor, Uncle Vanya, you're crying.

(through tears)

You've never known joy in your own life, but . . . you wait, Uncle Vanya, you just wait . . . We shall rest . . .

(embraces him)

We shall rest!

(The WATCHMAN taps. TELEGIN plays softly on his guitar. MARIA VASILYEVNA writes in the margin of her pamphlet. MARINA knits a stocking.)

We shall rest.

THE CURTAIN SLOWLY FALLS.

END OF PLAY.

www.ingramcontent.com/pod-product-compliance
Ingram Content Group UK Ltd.
Pitfield, Milton Keynes, MK11 3LW, UK
UKHW020237250726
13967UKWH00001B/425